This book is for everyone who w
to do something to help wild
N.E.

Thanks go to my family and friends for input and support.

Special shout out to James, Charlie, Ailsa, Brian, Claire, Catherine

and Amelia. Thanks also to Cressida Peever for her critiques.

To Charlotte

Nan Eshelby

Eshelby Publishing

First published in 2022 by Eshelby Publishing

Haverhill, Suffolk

ISBN 978-1-9168821-1-9

A catalogue record for this book will be available from the British Library

Text and Illustration Copyright © Nan Eshelby 2022

The right of Nan Eshelby to be identified as the Author and Illustrator of this work has been asserted by them in accordance with the Copyright Designs and Patents Act 1988

Printed in Suffolk by Leiston Press.

Maisie Daisy & Mo

Nature Books

PUDDOCK'S POND

Written & Illustrated by Nan Eshelby

Maisie, Daisy and Mo
were happily watching the
busy bees in their wildflower garden.
Mo looked up and saw that the
sky was getting gloomy and grey.
He groaned, "Oh, how annoying!
I think it is going to rain.
Come on, let's run to our den."

They sheltered
and stared at the rain.
Suddenly Maisie cried,
"Listen!" making them all jump.
A faint rustle!
A croak!

With wide eyes, Maisie, Daisy and Mo
saw a frog, wearing a lily crown,
slowly appear from the undergrowth.
"Oooh look!" Maisie exclaimed, jumping forward...

"Wait!" whispered Daisy,
"Frogs are shy creatures,
and we don't want to
frighten him."
"Just stand quietly,"
Mo suggested.
They stood still.
Time passed slowly.

Suddenly,
the frog jumped,
and
Maisie, Daisy and Mo

were so surprised
they jumped too.

"G-g-good day!"
the frog croaked hesitantly.
"M-m-my name is Puddock.
I do not normally speak to people,
but my friend Bombus the Bee
said you had helped him by
growing flowers and that
you might help me?"

"It's amazing to meet you
in all of your glory.
We'd be honoured to help,
so please tell us your story."

Maisie giggled,
"I made a rhyme!"

Puddock croaked,
"This lily crown is magic and helps me speak to you.
But when I talk to frogs, rhyming is what I do.
So, thank you for your rhyme;
it makes me feel at ease.
And if it is OK,
may we continue in rhyme please?"

Daisy smiled,
"Yes indeed,
please proceed!"

Puddock sighed,

"I am sorry to tell you a story so bleak,
Of frog families lacking water, causing them to get weak.
Water is critical for all wildlife you see,
Without it some can't start their own family."

Mo looked up at the pouring rain,
"Are you saying this isn't enough?
Please tell us how this can be making things tough?"

Puddock explained,
"Rain doesn't remain,
it drains quickly away.
Especially on a hot sunny day.
If you would help us
by building a pond,
frogs and all nature
could happily belong."

"I-I-I am not asking
for anything big.
You could use
an old basin
or line a hole
that you dig."

Puddock croaked,
"A pond will be brilliant for frogs, toads and newts,
dragonflies, pond skaters and damselflies too.
If you are patient and quietly wait,
then all kinds of wildlife will investigate."

"Foxes, hedgehogs and birds will all love a drink,

even if out of an unwanted old sink."

Maisie hopped with excitement,

"We helped Bombus the Bee
by planting wildflowers here.
Doesn't it look great?
We only planned it last year.
Let's dig the new pond
to go next to the flowers.
How glorious it will look,
and it wouldn't take hours."

Mo said,

"There are various items,

that we need to find:

A spade, plants and stones,

so it will take some time.

I'll ask teacher

if everything is okay,

And we'll try to re-use things

to get us on our way."

Daisy thought carefully and said,

"Insects and amphibians

will love our pond, I know.

But I need to learn more,

so we're ready to go."

Maisie called to Puddock,

"We know what to do, we have all that's required.

Let's start the pond now, we're not a bit tired."

Puddock croaked,

"I-I-I hope you don't mind,

but I must now hide,

as it is not safe for me

to be near a job site.

I'll go and bring more frogs.

That won't be too tough!

It's all so exciting,

I can't thank you enough."

Maisie, Daisy and Mo dug a hole,

nice and wide.

They put in the basin,

with stones round the side.

They filled it with water,
sparkling so bright.
Then added some plants
and the pond looked just right.

Maisie shouted,

"Puddock we've finished.

Please come out and look!"

Puddock happily hopped in,

"Thank you so much,

the pond is quite brilliant.

I've brought lots of frogs,

to come and jump in it."

Daisy asked Puddock,

"I know that our pond will help wildlife to thrive,

But what happens next, after wildlife arrives?"

Puddock grinned,

"As springtime approaches,
an exciting thing dawns.
Lots of black dots of
frog and toad spawn.
Then suddenly, all of the
spawn will be gone.
Next will come tadpoles –
it won't take too long."

Maisie, Daisy and Mo kept a watch by and by,
When they noticed the froglets had gone
and asked, "Why?"
Puddock croaked,
"When frogs grow large, they jump out and hide,
In dark and damp places in your garden, outside."

Mo looked up when
he heard a buzz overhead,
"Look who's flying in
from our new flower bed!"

"It's Bombus the Bee,"
they all cried with delight.

"I've drunk from your pond.
It's great – just right.
Maisie, Daisy and Mo
I'm so proud of you all.
Your pond will help wildlife,
no matter how small."

Maisie, Daisy and Mo say,
"We need to get children
to build ponds at home.
They'll need to have help –
they can't do it alone.
Let's all help each other
and so, lead the way.
Ask our teachers and parents
and see what they say.
It is all SO exciting
helping nature this way.
We ALL need to reach
out and spread the
message today."

Puddock says, "Thank you", to all of his friends
and that includes you for reading on to the end.
But don't be too sad, there is more at the back.
Puddock and friends have put in loads of great facts.
Finish the pond drawing I've left for you here.
Why not fill it with wildlife to bring you great cheer?

In this section of the book Maisie, Daisy, Mo and Puddock want to share some of their favourite facts. If you want to learn more there are lots of great sources on the web.

In this book, 'Puddock's Pond', the lead character is called Puddock and the drawing is based on a 'common frog' or to give the Latin name, '*Rana temporaria*' (try saying that 3 times very quickly!).

Puddock is a Scottish word used to describe frogs or toads. There is a wonderful poem by John M Caie called 'The Puddock' and I recommend reading it online.

When you come across any wildlife in your pond do watch, learn and enjoy but try and avoid disturbing them.

If you want to pick up a frog, toad or newt then ask an adult. Wash and thoroughly rinse your hands before and after. Frogs can absorb through their skin so they can get damaged if you have anything on your skin.

'Common Frog' Facts

Puddock is an amphibian. Amphibians are small vertebrates (animals that have a backbone) that require habitats with suitable breeding ponds.

Common frogs can be found in many parts of the world, including Europe, Asia and Americas.

They have smooth skin that varies in colour from grey, olive green and yellow to brown.

They have long legs for hopping and jumping as opposed to toads which prefer to walk and have shorter legs.

Common frogs can be found in many parts of the world, including Europe, Asia and Americas.

They have smooth skin that varies in colour from grey, olive green and yellow to brown.

Frogs have long legs for hopping and jumping as opposed to toads which prefer to walk and have shorter legs.

Common frogs hibernate during the winter in pond mud or under piles of rotting leaves, logs, or stones.

They can breathe through both their skin as well as their lungs.

Frogs are usually most active at night.

In spring male frogs croak to attract females. The male embraces a female and fertilises her eggs as she lays them in shallow water providing frogspawn.

Tadpoles emerge, and over about 14-16 weeks gradually change into froglets: a process known as metamorphosis.

Young tadpoles feed on algae. As they develop into adults, they eat insects that they catch with their long, sticky tongue.

Adults are described as carnivorous, this means they eat food such as insects, snails, slugs, and worms.

As you can see from the drawing of Puddock, there are 4 fingers at the front and 5 webbed toes at the back. The webbed toes help frogs to swim.

Common frogs have lengths of roughly 8-13cm (have a look on your ruler) and weights of around 22g (approximately 4 grapes) and an average lifespan of 5-10 years.

The world's smallest frog, identified in 2012, is 7mm (roughly the size of a garden pea) and was found in Papua New Guinea, which is off the coast of Australia.

They can slightly lighten or darken their skin to match their surroundings.

A group of frogs is called an army.

Frogs 'drink' water through their skin.

The world's largest frog species is known as the 'Goliath Frog' and lives in Western Africa and can grow to be around a 30cm (the length of a standard ruler) and weigh up to around 3kg (3 bags of sugar)- wow that is a BIG frog.

'Common Toad' Facts

There are quite a few things that
the common frog and toad have in
common, but two of the differences
which are obvious are their
skin and spawn.

The have dry warty skin, giving it
a lumpy appearance; and toad spawn
is in long strings (see pictures
inside this book).

It has already been mentioned
that toads have shorter legs
and prefer to walk than hop.
Toads can survive longer in
dry areas than frogs.

Newt Facts

If you look at the pond drawings in the book you will see newts and, in the UK, the most common newt is a 'smooth newt'.

If you are lucky and patient, you may get newts in your pond – they are quite private, but if you do see one, you will agree that they are very cute.

Smooth newts can grow to 10cm and are generally brown in colour.

The under belly is yellow/orange with small black spots.

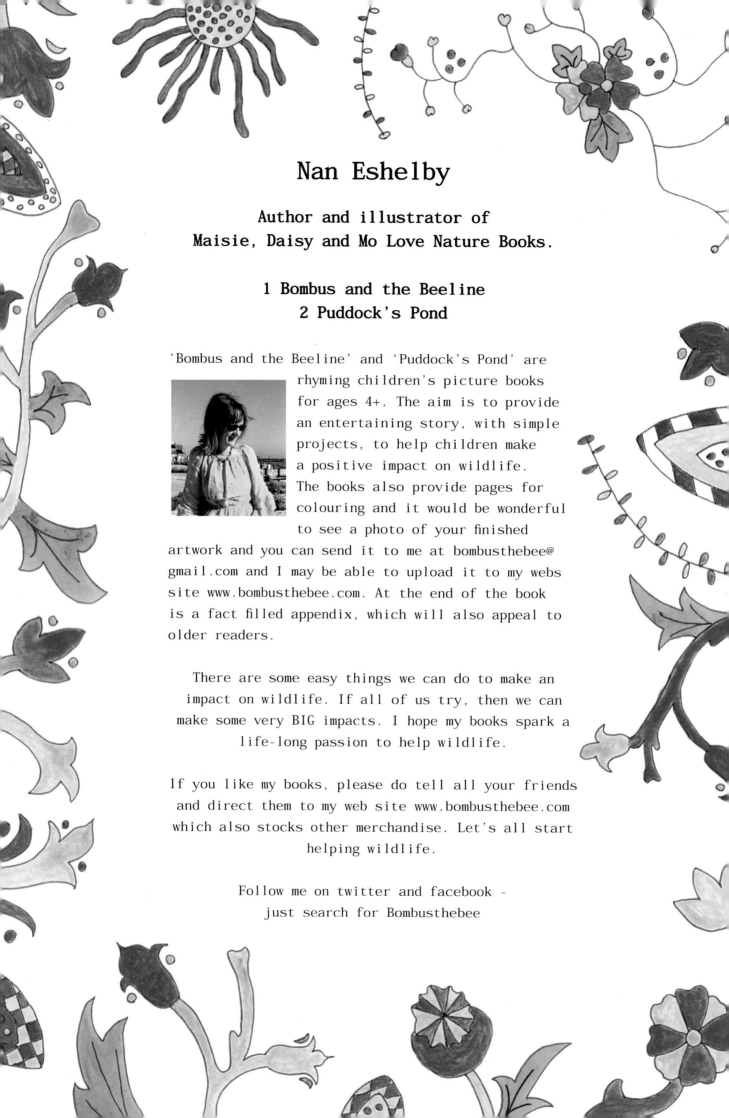

Nan Eshelby

**Author and illustrator of
Maisie, Daisy and Mo Love Nature Books.**

**1 Bombus and the Beeline
2 Puddock's Pond**

'Bombus and the Beeline' and 'Puddock's Pond' are rhyming children's picture books for ages 4+. The aim is to provide an entertaining story, with simple projects, to help children make a positive impact on wildlife. The books also provide pages for colouring and it would be wonderful to see a photo of your finished artwork and you can send it to me at bombusthebee@gmail.com and I may be able to upload it to my webs+ site www.bombusthebee.com. At the end of the book is a fact filled appendix, which will also appeal to older readers.

There are some easy things we can do to make an impact on wildlife. If all of us try, then we can make some very BIG impacts. I hope my books spark a life-long passion to help wildlife.

If you like my books, please do tell all your friends and direct them to my web site www.bombusthebee.com which also stocks other merchandise. Let's all start helping wildlife.

Follow me on twitter and facebook -
just search for Bombusthebee